FEAST FOR 10

CATHRYN FALWELL
CLARION BOOKS, NEW YORK

Clarion Books
a Houghton Mifflin Company imprint
3 Park Avenue, 19th Floor, New York, New York 10016
Text and illustrations copyright © 1993 by Cathryn Falwell
All rights reserved.

For information about permission to reproduce selections from
this book, write to trade.permissions@hmhco.com or to
Permissions, Houghton Mifflin Harcourt Publishing Company,
3 Park Avenue, 19th Floor, New York, New York 10016.
Printed in China

Library of Congress Cataloging-in-Publication Data

Falwell, Cathryn
Feast for 10 / by Cathryn Falwell.
p.   cm.
Summary: Numbers from one to ten are used to tell how
members of a family shop and work together to prepare a meal.
ISBN 0-395-62037-6   PA ISBN 0-395-72081-8
[1. Counting.   2. Afro-Americans—Fiction.   3. Cookery—Fiction.
4. Family life—Fiction.]   I. Title. II. Title: Feast for ten.
PZ7.F198Fe   1993
[E]—dc20
92-35512   CIP   AC

SCP   50   49   48
4500704067

For
my family

in
loving memory
of
my grandmothers

Willie Mae McMullen Chauvin
and
Evelyn Haning Falwell

who often made
feasts for plenty

1 one
cart
into the
grocery
store

 two
pumpkins
for pie

3 three
chickens
to fry

**4** four
children
off to
look for
more

5 five
kinds
of beans

6 six
bunches
of greens

 seven
dill pickles
stuffed in
a jar

 eight
ripe
tomatoes

9 nine
plump
potatoes

10 ten hands help to load the car

Then . . .

1 one
car
home
from the
grocery
store

2 two
will
look

3 three
will
cook

4 four will taste and ask for more

5 five
empty
cans

 six
pots and
pans

7 seven
more carrots
to wash
and
peel

8 eight
platters
down

9 nine
chairs
around

10 ten hungry folks to share the meal!

Career Day

I wonder what I'll be when I grow up.

Grown-ups sure have interesting work to do!
And so do we.

Today it's Mr. Siscoe's turn
to introduce his special visitor.
He says, "Good morning, everyone.
I'd like you to meet Professor Alcorn.
He's my teacher at college."
Hey—I never knew grown-ups
had teachers, too!

When it's time for Nicholas
to introduce his visitor, he says,
"I'll bet you've all bought groceries
at the Friendly Farm Market.
Guess what—my father is manager of the store."

Evan's father wears a leather apron
that holds the tools he uses all the time.
He shows us how to hammer a nail.

Sam's visitor drives the sanitation truck
that carries our garbage to the big town dump.
Kate and Eveline and I wave to him, just as
we always do whenever he comes down our street.
"Hey, kids—remember to recycle!" Sam's father says.

Jessica's mother takes care of animals.
She's a veterinarian, the kind of doctor
who makes sick animals better.

Eveline's mother is a nurse in the hospital.
She takes care of all the newborn babies in our town.
She tells us those babies are very, very cute,
but they sure do cry a lot when they're hungry.

Sarah's visitor is our crossing guard.
She brings Sarah to school every day,
because she is also Sarah's grandmother.
That's why Sarah is always the first one at school
and the last one to go home in the afternoon.

Mrs. Madoff's visitor is her husband.
He's a scientist called a paleontologist.
He just got back from South America,
where he was digging for dinosaur bones.
The bones tell us about dinosaurs
that lived long ago.

Michiko's mother writes books for us to read.
She draws the pictures in them, too.
She is very good at drawing mice.

When Kate introduces her visitor, she says,
"My dad plays bass in an orchestra at night.
He practices all day and takes care of
my baby brother while our mother goes
to work at the bank."

Next we meet Charlie's visitor.
His mother is a judge who works
in a courtroom and wears a long black robe.
If there's too much noise, she pounds her gavel
and says, "Order in the court!"
Then everyone has to be quiet.

Here he is—right on time!
"Uh, this is my dad," I say.
"He drives a big bulldozer.
He's helping build our new library."
"Good morning, Mr. Lopez," everyone says.
"Good morning, boys and girls," my dad says.

What if I forget what I'm supposed to say?
Sometimes that happens.
Not just to me, Mrs. Madoff says,
but to everyone.

Jessica CALENDAR   Sam JUICE

Michiko LEADER   Charlie LIGHTS

Nicholas WEATHER   Kate PLANTS

Eveline SNACK   Pablo FLUFFY

Evan RS   Sarah MAIL

When special visitors come to our school,
they tell us about the work they do.
Then we tell them about the work we do.
Today it's my turn to introduce my visitor.

For Christian and Sam,
who will grow up to do something wonderful.
—A.R. and L.R.

Career Day

story by **Anne Rockwell**   pictures by **Lizzy Rockwell**

SCHOLASTIC INC.

New York Toronto London Auckland Sydney
Mexico City New Delhi Hong Kong Buenos Aires

12 11 10 9 8 7 6 5 4   3 4 5 6/0

Printed in the U.S.A.   14
First Scholastic printing, October 2001